Bad Motel

Robert Scotellaro

ISBN: 978 0 9969887-6-6
Printed in the United States of America

Cover Art: Tom Brown
Back Cover Photo: Diana Scott

Also by Robert Scotellaro:

What We Know So Far (Blue Light Press, 2015)
Measuring the Distance (Blue Light Press, 2012)

Chapbooks

After the Revolution (White Knuckle Press, 2014)
The Night Sings A Capella (Big Table Publishing, 2011)
Rhapsody of Fallen Objects (Flutter Press, 2010)
My Father's Cadillac (Six-Shooter Press, 1984)
Early Love Poems of Genghis Khan (Lion's Breath Press, 1979)
Blinded by Halos (Lion's Breath Press, 1978)
East Harlem Poems (Vagabond Press, 1977)

Children's Books

Snail Stampede and Other Poems (Hands Up Books, 2004)
Dancing with Frankenstein and Other Limericks (Hands Up Books, 2003)
Daddy Fixed the Vacuum Cleaner (Willowisp Press, 1993)

Big Table Publishing Company
Boston, MA
www.bigtablepublishing.com

"No sunrise but the orange on the table;
pleasure in the form of a black dog. The spider's
red insistence collaborates with a yellow sponge
to form the morning's art."
                              —Christopher Kennedy

Acknowledgements

Grateful acknowledgement is made to the following publications in which these stories or earlier versions previously appeared:

"Maybe So" *100 Word Story*

"Erasure" *100 Word Story*

"Bad Hotel" *100 Word Story*

"A Change of Clothes" *100 Word Story*

"Air Harp Would Be Better" *Boston Literary Magazine*

"Duct Tape" *Boston Literary Magazine; The Best of Boston Literary Magazine Anthology*

"The Small End of the Funnel" *Microfiction Monday Magazine; Microfiction Monday Magazine's 2015 Anthology*

"What's Left" *Microfiction Monday Magazine; Microfiction Monday Magazine's 2015 Anthology*

"So They Said" *Microfiction Monday Magazine*

"Triple-Digits" *Flash: The International Short-Short Story Magazine*

"Smoke Signals" *Flash: The International Short-Short Story Magazine*

"Insect Oracles" *Flash: The International Short-Short Story Magazine*

"Sewn In" *Flash: The International Short-Short Story Magazine*

"Ballet, Sinus Headaches, and a Decent Steak" *Postcard Poems and Prose Magazine*

"Sonic Boom" *DOGZPLOT*

"Pareidolia" *Postcard Shorts*

"The Treachery of Windows" *Zone 3*

"My Father, King Kong, and I-90" *A Quiet Courage*

"Mannequins by Candlelight" *A Quiet Courage*

"Dust Devils in Multicolor" *A Quiet Courage*

Contents

What We Carry

What Remains

What If?

For Diana

What We Carry

Pareidolia

My sister sees an Eskimo in the inkblot markings of her old cat. "See?" she says. She's never spotted Jesus or Elvis in anything, and I'm grateful. She makes dollhouse furniture she sells at fairs and flea markets. Impeccable works little fingers will tirelessly rearrange. She lives small/works small. Is still pining over her first love. A lifeguard who peaked in high school. Works in a Kleenex factory. "Paper products," she says, "who doesn't need them?" We order pizza. Sit in front of the TV. All that melted cheese and sauce in a swirl. One could see just about anything.

Mannequins by Candlelight

"Gun for sale. Used only once," my wife said, reading another of her six-word stories. We were in the basement of the house her father left her. A tornado on the other side. Candle flames wobbled. Mannequin limbs reached out from boards and pipes. Material for the art her father never got to make.

"How can you?" I said.

"Helps me get my mind off things," she said.

"I like it," I told her. Grabbed a hand with curled fingers and scratched my back. Something large banged against the house and a mannequin toppled. I asked her to read another.

Air Harp Would Be Better

Yolanda hated it when he called her "Yo." He worked full-time for a florist despite his hay fever. She was writing a book about 1930s tearjerker movies called: *Weepers*. He'd bring home wilted lilies and yellow roses. Say: "Yo, where you want these?" The trash came to mind. He'd watch football and would shoot up when his team scored a touchdown, play air guitar. Hitting all the high notes with atonal screeches. She'd write a room away. Wanted a baby. They had two cats instead. Sometimes she'd watch them, crouched. The metronomic way they beat their tails against the rug.

The Interview

Sometimes Eric felt he was walking through a boxed canyon. With every likelihood of an ambush. His socks were gray, his suit, blue, and his tie had red stripes angled like whiplashes. The interview was on the top floor. Everything was riding on it. A young man beside him with his hat on backwards moved a toothpick around in his mouth like a baton to the Muzak. Eric wanted a hat like that to wear backwards. Someone old kept pressing the "Close" button at every stop, again and again and again and again. With no effect on the outcome, whatsoever.

Smoke Signals

My father would bring home fish, instead of flowers, after harsh words stained everything. My mother watching him from her plastic slipcovers, squeaking on the couch. Blowing cigarette smoke out, hard and fast, in dragon-streams. In a language more facile than words. He'd add the fish to her tropicals. A Kandinsky palette scattering into the water. Roll up his sleeve and reposition the castle, our castle, then pull his arm from the tank. "Your favorites," he'd say, snatching up some tissues and wiping up quickly. My mother's smoke coming out at him in smooth syntax then, thin and measured. Forgiving.

Big Fish/Little Fish

There was a miniature picket fence at the back of their trailer. A garden. Petunias. She wanted to go whale watching. Far away where there was a boat. An ocean, parting. That mighty surge. The bigness offsetting smallness. Said they could afford it. He was bald and had a closet full of hats. Wore them even in the house.

"I'll get you a goldfish," he said. Then laughed. Turned his baseball cap backwards, thinking it made him look years younger.

"I already have a goldfish bowl," she said. They didn't, and he wondered what the hell she could possibly mean.

Tay Ninh Dump

I'm an 18-year-old two-minute wonder. The whore is younger. Has a hook where a hand should be. We're in a cardboard structure. Flies from the dump storm the walls. "I ti-ti," she says, meaning she is tight. A standard line. She climbs on top. Outside, Banks is waiting. Itching to call me "hair trigger". The hook touches me. I eat a fly. I think: birds on fire, ice cream in my eyes. It doesn't help.

"I wait," I say.

"You go," she says.

I flash a bill. We sit there, sweating.

"Okay, Romeo," Banks says when I finally step out.

Erasure

Janelle still had her ex-pimp's name, over a smoking gun tattoo, peeking out of her blouse. *Property of "Stinger."* She had been out of the life for years. Many states away. Living in her brother's basement. Writing country songs she sang at the *Bottom Rung*. With a beer at her feet she lifted often. The bartender's name was Rusty. But he wasn't. She didn't know which of his lava lamps she liked best. He never asked about her tattoos. One night they went back and forth like kids. "Bet you can't"/ "Bet I can…" "Holy-goddamn-god-almighty," he said, when she did.

Baits Motel

It was actually called *The Baits Motel*. They sold worms there/fishing equipment. There was a lake nearby, where the desk clerk said the fish jumped into your boat. That you needed an umbrella. He smiled. There were teeth missing. We'd drive for days. Stop. Collect ourselves. Then drive on. What we left behind, we didn't. Some things grew in sand. In thin air. I needed a bartender's psychiatry. You, much less. The worms creeped us out. The crickets were cacophonous. You started smoking again. I watched your cigarettes blossom in the dark. Mosquitoes flew in the windows and never left.

So They Said

The chickens pecked around their steps as they headed back to the house. The sky lay low, brooding; charcoaled by rain. It would soon be more intimate. They'd just returned from an exorcism. A boy with one leg shorter than the other. Who didn't listen to his parents. Typed Satan-speak into his computer. Spoke sometimes in tongues. They said. All of them gathered around with *God-words*, and he told them to go fuck themselves. In a language they understood. They waited for the holy water to smoke and sizzle when it touched his skin. When it didn't, they headed home.

I Got Something

The stranger tapped at our fire escape window. My mother grabbed a kitchen knife and pulled the shade back. He had a long something wrapped in a blanket. He said through the glass: "Whitey said it was OK. I got something." Whitey was a gangster down the hall. My mother let him see the knife. He said, "Don't worry." She let him in. The rifle was placed under my bed. I was eight. Knew too much. Whitey came weeks later and handed Mom some money. There was just dust under my bed again. Then the winter came. Just like always.

The Treachery of Windows

We lived in a tenement, five floors from a hard kiss of cement—a bounce off clotheslines. A long scream, then silence. I pictured this each time my mother cleaned windows. Her back to the unobstructed air. Crumpled newspaper in one hand. Windex in the other. A rotted Victorian frame on her lap.

"Hold my legs," she'd say. My tiny form, her ballast. That tourniquet I became. "Not so tight," she'd say—a thin sheet of foaming glass between us. Then mouthing the words slowly, as though I might read her lips and relent. "Not...so...tight. *Not...so...tight.*" But I never listened.

Ballet, Sinus Headaches, and a Decent Steak

Sandra performed water ballet. Legs bending, twirling. There'd been talk of the Olympics. But her sinuses betrayed her. Those synchronized legs in a team photo, glistening. The machinery, she'd describe, at work below the art. I thought, isn't that the way it is? So many cogs even for the simplest graces. She married a butcher after we split up. He got her sinus meds. Watched films of her young legs breaking the pool water. Told me she was happy. Didn't miss any of it. I listened for machinery: clanking, hums. Didn't hear it. She said, the meat was always fresh.

Bataan Death March

Alice named all their animals after characters from the soap operas she watched. Even learned Spanish so she could add the Mexican ones to her list. Said, "You slay me," frequently, when her husband said something never intended to be at all funny. He was a dour man whose father had survived the Bataan Death March and never let him forget it. Leaving him to feel he was engaged in his own benign version through the years. Often, during sex, Alice called him by a different name. He wondered who the fuck Bret was. But never cared enough to ask.

Twenty Aerobic Country Hits

Maggie saw the woman in a black burka at the thrift store. Only her eyes showed. The woman was holding a small pink doll against her breast. Barbie in a dark night, Maggie thought. Jake was going through old LPs. "The Cadillac of suppression-wear," she whispered, pointing.

Jake flashed: *20 Aerobic Country Hits* at her. "Always thought a chastity belt was." He laughed.

When Maggie turned, the two women's eyes met. It was as if the woman peeked through a slit in a wall. Maggie recognized the gesture instantly.

"Break out them dancin' shoes," Jake said. Flashing the album again.

Lovely Bones

They were in a shoebox under her bed. Her Victorian dildo collection. Ivory, darkened through the ages. Prized bones excavated. I told her they were *lovely*. The wrong word perhaps, for they went back quickly underground. She had a bird that talked. Said: "My bad!" for no reason I understood. There was a framed photo of her ex on a large horse. "I hate you. Hate you," the bird said, and she stiffened. The wet bar was vintage and the bottles mirrored colorfully. I wanted to say "Lovely"—said "Cool" instead. A saxophone in stereo filled in everything else unspoken.

Gravitational Pull

At the skating rink we sat on the other side of the glass. With coffees. My glasses fogging, then clearing, fogging again. The way my life did. A seven-foot giant at the center of the ice was spinning, his arms in the air, till he turned into a colorful blur. Everyone skated around him as though in orbit. "I wrote a six-word story," my wife told me. Read it from a napkin. "Six words prior were his last," she said. "Wow," I said, and she flipped the napkin over. Put a pen to it. Funny, I thought, these things: *orbits.*

The Small End of the Funnel

P.S. Brenda's doing Phone Sex. Can you believe it? I remember her saying the word "robust" once. It was hot.

P.P.S. Kay's into photography now. Close-ups of rusty staples in phone poles. Rain shadows trickling down a wall. Artists. Christ.

P.P.P.S. I called Brenda the other night. And man oh man!

P.P. P. P.S. Out of nowhere Kay says, "All cheaters should be pushed down a funnel with the small end in hell." I looked at her like, that's interesting. Like, there's nothing in <u>this</u> fridge worth taking. Only began breathing again when she started taking pictures of the cat.

Bad Motel

The cab driver's eyes in the rearview mirror as our lips parted. Lowering, when my eyes were added.

Too much to drink. The motel ceiling fan spinning the scarf you tossed up there. It was red and green. And it wasn't even Christmas. Just felt that way.

Watching TV, after. A politician. A lot of double-talk. You shook your head. Said, "What does it matter if the devil paints his kitchen white?"

On the way back, you told me your husband's hands were softer than my own.

In the light rain, our taxi veered around a mattress in the road.

Unlikely Oracles

Spiders were everywhere. In the linens, in the tub, still as stains or crawling up and sliding back down. In the lumpy terrain of our sock drawers. Swinging out into the fall rain from umbrellas popped open. It was the year my father died. That raccoons nearly killed our dog. There was coyote spray for the raccoons. Nothing for my father. Soon after he passed they vanished. Then the ants came. Fountains of them. From undiscovered places. Lines of them like fractures. The ant traps were sticky, like life was sticky. Sprays burned our eyes. We wondered what was next.

What We Carry

One of the things his father left him in his will was a sledgehammer. We were at an old-timer's bar. No frills, just some cartoon napkins and a barkeep with a rag in perpetual motion.

"A ten pounder," he said. "With most of the paint missing. I wondered if it was supposed to mean something. You know—*deep*. Like some things need to be busted down in order to build them better."

"Probably just something he wanted you to have," I said. Wished I hadn't.

"Yeah..." he said, running a finger through a wet circle, turning it into something else.

Sewn In

Outside the diner it was raining. Periodically, a truck's air brakes would add its hiss to the mix. The trip had been tough. Talk, cracked as some of those roads. There were miles yet. Rain shadows ran down that dress you got in Mexico. Little mirror pieces sewn in. You said, "We are all prisoners of our own momentum." I passed the salt. Didn't know what else to do. The waitress poured coffee like she invented it. Had a wet rag that did little more than reconfigure the table grease. When she flipped her pad page over, we looked up.

Duct Tape

My father thought duct tape could fix anything. He used it to pat us
down for lint, to block the tub's overflow, so the bath water reached
our chins—on lawn furniture and frayed wires, baring their orange
teeth, keeping us safe. And finally, those fractured years, a kind of
duct tape he tried on his marriage—dust and booze undoing its
sticking power. The deafening sound of it pulled from the roll, again
and again. Each new piece cut with his teeth, never holding. Better
served for those broken taillights and garden hose leaks, where its
magic never failed.

WHAT REMAINS

My Father, King Kong, and I-90

There was a photo of my father slid into my dresser mirror for years. Hair slicked back and big. Posed in front of a carnival bust of King Kong on *his* dresser. A cigarette in its mouth. I still have it. Somewhere. Amidst the basement dust. What we become, he became.

Pulled up, when I was little, in a long blue Cadillac to drop off Christmas presents. A ray gun. A blender that never worked right. Then sped off for good. Those beautiful and terrible taillight fins. A shark's. No longer circling. Slicing away instead, through those easy highway miles.

Hemingway in a Wetsuit

A nerd in college, he was swimming in tech money now. Had a large house out by the beach. Was into surfing. I'd given him his first joint (which freaked him out). He was paying me back by showing off now. Had a roomful of big game taxidermy. Store bought no doubt. Claws/teeth. Some kind of overcompensating Hemingway syndrome. Creepy as hell. "Want a brew?" he said. Had a refrigerator filled with high end labels. Later, he came out in a wetsuit. He was the same chubby guy I knew. Even in black. I watched the waves knock him around.

Triple-Digits

He was a foreman in a toaster factory. Kept bringing them home. The kitchen counter had three. The rest, stored in the basement. *Wedding gifts*, he'd tell her. The day the divorce papers came through, she tossed them all: a clunky can full. There'd been triple-digit heat for nearly a week, and thinking of them made her even hotter. She blasted some rap her father would have called *sin music*. Stood in her bra and panties in front of the refrigerator with the door open. With no one to complain about her, *letting the cold air escape*. Escapes were good.

Critical Putts

Glen speaks softly as though talking on a golf green during a critical putt. Even in the noisy bar. Even after his fifth drink, and someone on TV hits a homerun and the barkeep turns the sound up. Glen's talented fingers around a bottle or a glass. Teaching kids how to tickle the ivories now, as they elephant-walk across them and a metronome ticks away the hours. Who once played Carnegie Hall. To a packed house. Bartok shuddering under his attacks. Sings: "Born To Be Wild" on Karaoke Night. So softly we all have to turn an ear. Lean in.

An Accounting

She dragged him off to Bingo. Citing how great it'd be to do it together. Thirty-two years in Accounting and now she'd have him drowning in numbers again. Numbers with none of the elegance or mystery he'd known. Each time she marked a square, she'd brighten. There was a time it took a hotel in Rio. *Christ*, the bikinis she popped out of... He recalled that in feudal Japan, they had soldiers whose only duty was to count the number of severed heads after every battle. When I-9 was called, she elbowed him—stabbed a finger at his unblemished card.

Subtraction and Addition

My father was a gravedigger for a time. And I'd think, how depressing. To part the earth for others. But he didn't seem to mind. Had his beer, his TV, his racing pigeons on the roof. And the earth was merely a matter of subtraction and addition with boxes in-between. Just boxes.

I helped his new wife in the garden. She was a digger too, but there was always resurrection there. Her hyacinths rising up. Snipped for the table. For the eyes/the nose. Then the compost later in a droop. And then the roses—redder for it. All that math.

Bad Boy Pinwheel

It was a swastika tattoo he converted to a pinwheel. Black and blue with prison smears of red. On a taut bicep below his rolled up sleeve. A bit more ink was all it took. A tattoo parlor fond of bluebirds and roses. My sister's bad boy boyfriend. "He's saved," she says. "Shaved head and balls and shaved of sin." Gets a kick out of that. "Saved" and "shaved." "Hell is Heaven's jailhouse," he told me once. Laughing without his eyes involved. That pinwheel spinning in the TV light. My sister blowing on it, so hard you felt the wind.

New Light

If their leader said he could lasso a fly from the air with dental floss, she'd believe him. Drove those long miles to the desert. *New Light* they called themselves. She sounded different on the phone. Said it would be the last I'd hear from her. How she didn't miss TV, booze— any of it. Something metaphysical about "potholes." Hoped Baxter, her old Pomeranian (mine now) wouldn't be much bother. Baxter was happily licking his balls. When I told her, and she didn't laugh (that huge laugh that made the house bigger) I realized I'd been speaking to her ghost.

Into the Wires

There was a tuba against the wall in the guest room one of the kittens kept jumping into. The kids were grown. The tuba player played sweeter notes now, worlds away. The kittens bit into the wires. There were lots of wires. Lot of kittens. They peed on the rug. Clawed at her furry slippers. Madge got Jim hand warmers for his arthritis that looked like oven gloves. He'd put in the microwave then wear. She smiled when he put them around her waist. They collected Chia Pets: sprouting animals, leafy heads of hair. Overwatered. Always dripping. "Oxygen," she'd say.

What Remains

She tells me she saw shadows on the wall. What looked like robots in top hats. She's been hitting the morphine pump pretty good. Says, watching that small TV is like looking at a rock in a snowstorm. And would I tap some salt on her tongue. Those packets. Wants to feel the tang. *Something. Anything other...* That tongue that taught English Lit to troubled teens. Hemingway's big fish in ruin. The catcher in that chest high rye, catching. A tongue that wags at nurses flying by. "Now the sugar," she says. Points. Sticks her tongue out at me again.

A Sky Full of Wings

They were in her darkroom and she was pinning up photos of birds she'd taken. Mostly in flight. The wet rectangles were a night sky full. He told her he'd always wanted to be shot out of a cannon.

"Maybe you've got a *sperm complex*," she said.

"Like The Great Zantucci or something," he said, ignoring her. "Eyes following my arc of flight." She squinted, noticed for the first time the hawk had something in its talons. "Haven't you ever wanted to fly?" he asked. She gazed at him. The red light making both of them look a little strange.

Tin Ear

Outside the Vatican, they were waiting for the white smoke to spiral to the heavens. For a new Pope chosen. For God, the angels, the world to see. Vince watched on television. A tattoo of the Virgin Mary stretched across his chest. A scar down the front of her. Silvia, swept up in sex talk, had her client climaxing on speaker in the next room. Vince had a bad ear from the war and sometimes heard things funny. After, she said, "That makes three calls." He said: "Who has three balls?" She shook her head, showered. The smoke was black.

Fish Face and the Tap Dancing Man

My father said he saw a man once on the side of the road tap dancing in a ditch. We were watching TV in his nearly empty apartment. A fish tank between us his brother was picking up the next day. This move would be his last. I looked for a ditch in the movie we were watching. There wasn't any. Fish became part of his face. He held up his bottle. We toasted. I didn't know what. Deep in the blue sand was a castle. I wanted to live in one just like that when I was a kid.

A Change of Clothes

Widows are beautiful, he thought. So covered in need they shimmered. This was his third. She lay under a sheet, which had a hole burnt into it earlier from a pot seed exploded from a joint. The size of a lizard's eye. "His suits suit you," she said. "A little tight in the shoulders, but not so bad." Her cat rubbed against him, as if nothing had changed. He turned this way and that in the long mirror. Reached for a silk suit on a hanger. She rolled another, using a credit card to separate the seeds out this time.

Fog and Grit

He was never one to feather dust a cyclone, but rather, met it head on. His blue-collar body—rough hands into fists. The way he was. Sanded down now by fog and grit in this final storm. In his late eighties, on a kiddy ride outside the sprawling market. A smiling pink pig with much of the paint missing. The flip flop of big hands/little hands. His great granddaughter putting in a coin. A gentle rocking. A minute's worth. The pig sheathed in his long plaid jacket. He swam in now. Grabbing its ears. The girl smiling. The pig smiling.

His Decoys

In the casket Ben looked better dressed than Fran had seen him in years. Half expected him to pop up. Head down to the basement. Carve another of those stupid ducks. His lap too hot to handle, watching their teenage daughter's friends in short skirts, blooming out of halter tops. Watching him watching. Shuffling off to carve another. Dozens, no hunter would ever see. His redirected urges sanded down and painted. With truncated necks. On a shelf above some bicycles.

Fran's: "Thank you for coming..." And from the back, her daughter's friend texting. Muffling a giggle. Someone turning, saying: "*Shh.*"

Teen Mom

Her son draws children without mouths, even his clay snowman: every other feature in place but that fingernail curl where it should be. She thinks of herself his age; her blabbing Barbies with her cartoon voices. Her own lips sewn shut otherwise; her father looking down, frowning from the couch—is she him, without the pencil mustache? Later, when they make paper airplanes, hers dive straight down at her bare feet, and he laughs: a mouth now. His, sail across the room, stabbing into things. One, crash-landing in the closet. Into a candy apple red high heel she never wears.

HAZMAT

She said, as her teen came in to the house from that car parked in the dark down the street, that she smelled *sex on her*. Nearly emptied a can of hair spray (the first thing handy) over her, as though she had been exposed to something toxic, and her mother was working for HAZMAT. Her daughter covering her face, coughing. The spray burning both their eyes, as the daughter screamed something filled with *fucks!* and the dog barked at the two of them. And the mother said: "That mouth!" While just outside, a car beeped lightly as it passed.

Sonic Boom

"An airplane is like a blister on the heavens," he said, looking up. "Get a grip," she said. "This garden isn't going to plant itself." There were two saplings angled against the fence, a wheelbarrow filled with perennials. He picked the trowel up, plunged it into the soil. Some personalities were so large they dispersed another's language altogether, he thought. Left it to languor in the lungs. She handed him some bulbs. "How deep do you want these holes?" he asked. She demonstrated without speaking. And when she turned, he noticed her shadow fill an empty bucket to the brim.

Black & White

It was the best of times, it was the worst... A pause before my father's precipitous undoing. We were surrounded by his antique TV collection. Diminutive screens in stately console furniture. Dead eyes in every corner. We were both a little drunk. He'd inherited an old Chihuahua from a friend that passed. It kept farting and my father kept lighting matches.

"I wish they worked." He pointed. The TV he had that *did* work was in black and white. The way he always saw things. Nuance was the enemy. The pipes knocked and he turned. "It's nothing," I told him.

WHAT IF?

Her Hair in Freefall

"Imagine," he said, "there are caves *underwater* filled with air you can breathe." They were stopped at the top of the Ferris wheel. She gazed out at the ants below with cotton candy and grease-soaked edibles. The sounds: screams, laughter, wheels, velocity. "Imagine," he went on, "that small tabernacle of trapped air—waiting. How cool is that?"

She thought: starfish stuck to boulders. She thought: bubbles in ascension. She thought: Big Tony's Corvette. High above the waves, around curves with the top down. No goggles and plenty of air, untrapped, blowing her hair every which way. She thought: *Hell yes!*

Dust Devils in Multicolor and
That Shifting Moment

I got her a book called *The Secret of Cooking for Cats*. "I already know the secret," she said. "A can opener." I laughed. But felt a little hurt too. She had four cats. They twirled around her like small dust devils always looking to eat.

She worked from home. Designed patterns for children's mittens. Snowmen and Christmas trees were big around the holidays. I told her I'd always preferred gloves with fingers. "What about a little mystery?" she said, giving me *a look*. "What might be *underneath*?" She was a friend. Just that. I'd thought. Till that very moment.

Fat Shadows

The wind seemed to blow the crows from the trees. Their fat shadows painting the house as they passed. You said it was *a sign*. "I don't believe in signs," I said. But did. As a child, I wanted to be the one who called the countdowns for NASA. The drama in that reliable cadence before something monumental happened. We went inside, cooked a stew. To warm our bones as the windows rattled. There was always something rattling. Some kind of countdown. You cut carrots with a noisy knife against a board. I was careful not to spill the salt.

Ex Champ

In the corner the boxer wiped blood on his glove. His trainer slapped him. "Wake the fuck up! Use your left for Chrissakes." The boxer nodded. It was his kid's birthday and he wanted to be opening presents. Watching cartoons with him. He'd peaked years ago. Knew it. The cut man was working furiously. These young punks on his heels. Quick and hungry, knew nothing of the body's betrayal. Of the air, thick as bricks, that could no longer fit in your lungs. Couldn't care less about a kid in a birthday hat. The potbelly he looked forward to having.

Naturally

She didn't wear makeup. Not anything. Not ever. Said it was for clowns and opera singers. I liked her the way she was, but figured a little lipstick wouldn't hurt either.

She had stacks and stacks of travel magazines in her basement. They looked like stalagmites. Or stalactites down there in that cave. I could never remember which was which. All those lands pressed together she'd never visit. I noted how smooth her legs were—clean shaven. I said nothing. On TV (a talent show) a man juggled chain saws. "I can't look," she said, looking. I was looking too.

In the Sweet By and By

Between now and the Rapture he figured he'd fuck anything with a heartbeat. She was on her stomach. Piano keys tattooed down the length of her. Every note. "Play something," she said. He thought: church music. *In the Sweet By and By.* She: Jerry Lee Lewis. *Great Balls of Fire.* Told him she spent time in the "Nervous hospital." Said she'd seen a Hunky Jesus Contest once in Golden Gate Park. He wasn't sure he wanted to know what that was. Only when she said, "Something punchy," and arched up high against his fingers, did he begin banging the keys.

Out of the Office

With her arms around him, she leaned in, said: "Faster!" It was a Vespa not a Harley, but this was as close as they'd get to flying. He veered, full throttle, into the oncoming lane, cut in between two cars as a truck whooshed by. He had a glow-in-the-dark condom he was going to spring on her later. Have her close her eyes. She'd be ready. He pulled out again, cocked his wrist back hard. The wind was in their clothes, pulling out the workweek's dead things and flinging them. You could hear them slap against the road and break.

Maybe So

Ben likes saying, "What a revoltin' development *this* is," when Claire says something off-putting. From an old TV show he saw once. It annoys Claire, so he stops himself midway. They're in the Statue of Liberty. He thinks to mention how good it feels being inside this great lady. Means it in the best way. But doesn't. When they first met she said he looked like a biker-on-a-moped kind of guy. They gaze out from her crown. Heads in the clouds. He wonders what the torch might be like. The pinnacle. A metaphor that didn't burn perhaps. Or maybe did.

Random Study

The sky seems broader, the walls further apart. Chest pumping cleaner air deeper. He is taking a placebo and does not know it. No longer minds his dog shedding on the couch. When he hears his grandkids speak in acronyms, he does not think: WTF? Thirty-three years in Light Fixtures. Every shape and style, brand of brightness. Maybe now the light has finally clicked on. Is at the end of the tunnel. He washes his cereal bowl in the metal sink. Hears music in that small waterfall. The beach glass on the sill: a different length for each green shadow.

Llamas and Lloyds

They dream of owning a llama farm in California.

"Stately creatures," he says. "Two l's back-to-back. Now what's going to top that?"

"What about Lloyd?" she says.

"A herd of Lloyds. Now there's a thought."

***

On the weekends she sells off their noir movie collection. From his trunk he sells his adult movies for little gain.

***

He told her once, as a kid he'd steal his mother's dentures to use for leverage. Wished he hadn't. They look at mountains in the distance from their porch. See things. A Rorschach test game they play. When they can't, they make stuff up.

In the Drink

She told him there was a tribe in Africa that tied a cord around a father's testicles during childbirth. How the woman would pull the cord during the worst contractions. "Simpatico," she said. "They were in it *together.*" He winced. They were on the lake. One paddle in the water. She wore a bright yellow sundress and her belly hardly showed. He sang a rap song. Something about a long car, a fine booty, and a lot to give. One of his that never made it. Unlike the others.

"Stop that," she said, glaring

"Baby," he said. "Baby, baby, baby."

60 Feet

He'd never been athletic, no matter how she pushed him as a kid. Yet he turned out to be. She wasn't surprised when he went Goth—he was always different. But the black nail polish and all that makeup and facial jewelry, really threw her. And the call—that last call—his whining litany/that *filthy language*—who could blame her for slamming down the phone? 60 feet, they said—60 feet he climbed to the top of that beautiful Santa Barbara palm with a length of cord between his teeth, just enough—just enough to get the last word in.

Open Ended

Jen's words were freight only steel wheels could carry. Mine were made of something else. "It could be fun," she said. "You could. I could. What we have is strong enough." We were sitting on the roof. There was a snake in the cookie jar. Would always be. Some things changed everything that followed. An inch here, there, and parallel lines widened to infinity. She smiled. Full. I wanted it lopsided, doubt-sloppy. "I can't," I said. Only that. Stars were stars a moment earlier. Now they were shotgun holes in faux velvet. A bare light bulb on the other side.

Lincoln Gets Lucky

After the costume party he kept the top hat and beard on during sex. When she pulled the beard and the elastic band snapped it back, he said, "What the hell?" But she did it again and again till they got it right. Once they'd tried dirty talk with sock puppets. Gumming each other playfully. But this was better. A new elasticity.

"Routine can be a painful orbit," she said afterwards. He was a banker, was acquainted with the stern parenting of numbers. The trepidation in their exactness.

"Eight," he said.

"What?"

"Eight times you snapped that thing," he said.

Mike the Bike

Jeff decided he'd make up a god (a lesser god) and pray to it. He called his god, Mike, and figured He was teased as a kid: "Mike the bike...Mike the bike..." Before becoming a god. Mike, he decided, read *Popular Mechanics* and minds (Jeff's in particular) and had little to no influence on the Fates, or the intractable borders which separated one from their aspirations. But was a good listener. And that counted for a lot. For a good ear was worth a thousand tongues. And lord knew, thought Jeff, there were plenty enough of those to go around.

Inside and Out

Jake's cellmate says he believes in past lives. Says, "If you make fun of me, I'll rip your lungs out." Jake is looking through the sliver of window at a bird on the wall, inches from razor wire. Thinking: Genghis Khan, Vlad the Impaler…

His celly is washing his socks in a toilet scrubbed to a sheen. Rings them out. "A camel breeder," he says. " In the desert." Smiles. "This gal I was seein' told me. She was straight-up psychic."

"Wow," Jake says, wanting to make a joke about humps. Doesn't. The bird flies off into all that sky.

What If?

Not particularly religious, she hedged her bets. "Prayers-lite," she called them. Low expectation beseechments. A cross-your-fingers, tip-of-the-hat-to-heaven. In Nam I prayed to a sky I felt was empty, except for monsoon rain that never stopped. But did it anyway. Sat beside a toilet bowl when I got back just to hear it flush—again and again. It had been so long. A friend made it to the second round on a game show. My girlfriend closed her eyes, clasped her hands together. It was an old TV and in the dark, I liked the way it made the walls look.

A Room Full of Static

My girlfriend bid on a storage locker. Won a trunkful of transistor radios. For months each room was filled with static. Added to our own. I was working at a zipper factory back then. So many teeth opening and closing. She took a workshop, was reading my palm by the window. Lines in the skin I used to hold things. Roads and road signs she saw. "Ooh," she said and traced a finger along one. "What?" I said, but she didn't say. It was twilight and through the window glass, I could hear a jump rope slapping against the walk.

Nothing in the Fridge

There were peacocks on her property. Their screechy cries, inelegant. That spray of tail feathers making up for it. He told her he was "tuned in" to animals. Could read their thoughts somehow. Thinking that would curry favor. She asked what Edgar (her fat calico) was up to. Said, that time he peed in her slipper was the only time she heard him loud and clear. "It's not like that," he said. "Not like opening the fridge and grabbing something. It's kinda subtle." She stared at him and he turned. A peacock jumped a fence, fanning its plumes. He listened.

Domino Effect

He wanted to show off his karaoke skills at *his* place. She, an amateur toppler, wanted to show him the miniature Stonehenge she'd painstakingly positioned, winding through her kitchen. Compromising, they watched it fall—a synchronized, clicking moment's art into collapse. He did some supple James Brown moves amongst the rubble. Singing "I Feel Good" into an upturned rum bottle. Stripped, they rolled and grunted in the clutter. Tried counting the dot imprints, after, in each other's backs. Deciding they were too faint (the dots) and they were too drunk (the lovers) to make anything of them before they vanished.